Sally Nicholls

Shadow Girl

Barrington Stoke

With many thanks to Sarah Dodd

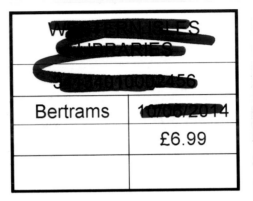

First published in 2014 in Great Britain by
Barrington Stoke Ltd
18 Walker Street, Edinburgh, EH3 7LP

www.barringtonstoke.co.uk

ISBN: 978-1-78112-313-3

Printed in China by Leo

Contents

1. BEFORE WE BEGIN

So, look.

This story is going to sound strange. I can't help that. I can only tell you what happened.

This is the story of how, when I was 14, I met a woman who'd known me for 20 years.

It's the story of how I lost one friend and found another.

It's the story of how I found a home.

Are you ready?

Let's begin.

2. LOST

The story begins with a horrible day. That wasn't unusual. I hated school. I'd been at my new school for two months, and I still hated it. All of the other kids had been there for years. They had people to sit with, and people to be partners with, and people to hang out with at break. I had no one.

I knew I should try to make friends, but I couldn't be bothered. There was no point – I'd be moving on soon. I was 14, and this was my third secondary school. I was in foster care – and I kept having to move. I'd lived in five different homes so far, in four different towns. You'd think

2

someone might want to keep me, but no one ever did.

It was better if I didn't make friends. It would make it easier when I had to go.

The reasons my day was so horrible were:

1. Catherine and Jade, who sat behind me in Maths and French. And were complete cows. And who thought it was funny to take the piss out of my shoes, and my bag, and my coat, and my hair, and anything else they could think of. It wasn't funny. It was pathetic.

2. Lunch. Or rather, the fact I didn't have anyone to sit with at lunch. It was like there was this arrow pointing at my head, with LOSER written on it. I wished I had the willpower to be anorexic. It would have made lunchtimes a lot easier.

3. Homework. Homework and me didn't get on. Homework thought I didn't put enough effort into our relationship and I thought homework always asked too much from me. Probably we were both right. Homework was another

thing I couldn't be bothered with. It meant I got put in detention a lot, but I didn't care. I would rather be in detention than stuck on my own with no one to talk to.

4. The school bus. The school bus was the worst bit of my whole day. I hated it. It was full of loud, silly boys and loud, silly girls. Kids were always throwing things or shouting things or breaking things. The bus driver just sat at the front and pretended he couldn't hear. You could have murdered someone and he wouldn't have stopped. He wouldn't even have made you clean up the blood.

When I got on the bus that day, the boys were in a silly mood.

"Clare!" they yelled when they saw me.

"Hey, Clare, will you be my girlfriend?"

"Is that your granny's coat, Clare?"

"Who cut your hair, Clare – a werewolf?"

Giggle, giggle, giggle.

"Do you go to a werewolf hairdresser, Clare? Awooo!"

And all the boys started making werewolf noises. The bus driver didn't even look round.

"Cla-are! I'm talking to you!"

So, you know how sometimes you just lose it?

I lost it.

"Shut up!" I said. I grabbed the biggest boy and slammed him into the side of the bus. The other kids went, "Ooooh!"

"Oooh, Clare!"

"Fight!"

"Fight! Fight! Fight! Fight!"

I guess I was wrong about that bus driver. He let those boys yell stuff at me for two months. But the one time I did something about it?

He threw me off the bus.

I was so angry. OK, so I might have yelled some stuff at him when he told me to get off. I might have told him he was stupid and pathetic and sexist and ugly. The other kids might have acted like this was the funniest thing they'd ever seen.

I stamped off down the road. I hated that stupid bus driver. I hated those boys. I hated them all.

I got to the end of the street and stopped. I'd never walked home from school before. I couldn't remember if the bus turned left here, or right.

I turned right. I kept walking.

The road ended. Left or right? I turned left. More streets. More houses. Dull, ordinary streets with dull, ordinary rows of houses. Streets that looked exactly the same as every street near where I lived.

Another road. Left? Or right? I kept walking. Left or right? I turned left. I kept walking. I walked, and walked, and walked, even though I knew it was hopeless.

I was lost.

3. THE WAY HOME

I stopped. I was beginning to panic. How was I going to get home? I couldn't call my foster mother, Lyn. I didn't have a mobile. Jade and Catherine had jumped up and down on it because I'd called them greasy mingers. Lyn said it was my own fault, and she wouldn't get me another one.

There was a phone box at the end of the street, but I didn't know Lyn's mobile number. And I couldn't call her at work. She was a journalist for the local newspaper. She was always charging around the countryside to go to school fêtes, and animal shows, and to interview local celebrities. She could be anywhere.

What was I going to do?

At first I was just scared. Then I got angry. This was all those boys' fault. And that stupid bus driver. I wanted to scream. So I did.

"Aaargh!" I yelled. "Aaargh!"

Then I noticed something.

Someone was watching me.

It was a girl, about my own age. She looked a bit familiar. Like I'd seen her somewhere before. But she didn't go to my school. Our school uniform was purple. This girl was all in green – green skirt, and a green tie. Her coat looked even older than mine. She had thick, dark hair that needed cutting, and a tiny purple bruise on her jaw. It gave her pale face a sort of lopsided look.

"What?" I said. "I'm just screaming at thin air. Haven't you ever screamed at thin air before?"

"Lots of times," the girl said. She came a bit closer. "Can I help?"

"I just got thrown off the school bus," I told her.

"Oh," she said. "That sucks. But it's not the end of the world, is it? You've still got legs."

"Well, yes," I said. "But I don't know how to get home. And I don't know my foster mother's phone number."

Uh-oh. I shouldn't have said foster mother. That always puts people off.

But the girl didn't look freaked out. She smiled.

"My name's Maddy," she said. "But don't make jokes about how mad I am. It's not funny. Are you in care? I am too. I live in a children's home. Not far from here."

And she waved her arm off somewhere to the left.

"My name's Clare," I said. "I used to live in a children's home. I hated it."

"Mine's awful," Maddy said. She looked sad for a moment, then she smiled. "How old are you? I'm 14. What's your street called? I might know where it is. Is it near the shops? Or the park? Or ..." She stopped. "Sorry. I mean, maybe I can help. If you'd like me to."

"I'd like you to," I said. "Oh God, I'd love you to help. Please, help! I live on Church Road. It's near the park. I know my way from the park. And I'm 14 too."

"OK," Maddy said. "I can get you to the park. Follow me!" And she set off, back the way I'd just come. Oops.

As we walked, Maddy talked. She talked a lot. I didn't mind. I'm pretty quiet, so I like noisy people. I like that they do the talking for me. Also, I could see Maddy was pretty nervous. She was worried I wouldn't like her, I could tell. Normally, that really puts me off someone. But today it just made me calmer. I knew Maddy wasn't going to be like Jade and Catherine and those boys on the bus. I liked that she wanted me to like her.

"I love your bag," Maddy said. "I've never seen a bag like that before. It's cool. How long have you lived here? What school do you go to? My school's awful. I hate it. All the kids are awful. Is yours the same?"

I wanted to laugh, but I didn't.

"Yeah," I said. "My school's awful. The school bus is even worse. Hey, I know where this is!"

I did, too. There was the park. There was the fish and chip shop. I was about five minutes' walk from Lyn's house.

"Listen," I said. "Thanks."

"No problem," said Maddy. "Um. You don't live that far from me. I'm ..." and she flapped her arm off to the left again.

"Maybe we could meet up sometime?" I said. Maddy beamed.

"Oh yes!" she said. I was smiling too. It was a long time since I'd made anyone look so pleased.

"What's your phone number?" I asked. Maddy looked at me like I was crazy.

"I live in a children's home," she said. "You can't just call!"

"You don't have a mobile?" I said.

"No." She looked a bit uncomfortable. I waited for her to explain, but she just said, "I've got to go now. Meet me at the bandstand after school tomorrow?"

"OK," I said.

Maddy beamed again. "Cool," she said. "OK. Great. Good. See you tomorrow."

4. LYN

I had been in care since I was seven. Half my life.

People always think that I must have had some terrible abusive family, but I didn't. I used to live with my mum and my dad, but my dad looked after me. Then when I was six my dad died, and when I was seven my mum went to prison. I haven't seen her since. She wasn't very interested in kids, my mum. That's what my gran says.

My gran's brilliant. I love my gran. I wish I could live with her, but she's really old and a bit bonkers. She lives in an old people's home down south. She never remembers my birthday, so she just sends me really, really bonkers presents any time she thinks of me. Sometimes they're brilliant, like the spud gun she gave me when I was nine, or the little stone hedgehog that used to belong to my dad. That's my favourite thing in the whole world. I keep it in a pocket in my schoolbag so I can take it out when I'm sad and remember my gran, and my dad, and what he was like. It's my most special, most secret thing. I told a kid about it once, and she stole it from my pocket. It took my foster mother months to find it again. So now I don't tell anyone. That was a present, but sometimes Gran gives me stuff that's utterly mad. Once she sent me six bottles of mineral water, in case there was a nuclear war. Another time, I got an Easter egg in November.

I also have a half-brother, Matt, who lives with his dad. Matt's 17. He's cool, but he's a bit of a boy. If I send him a text, he'll reply, but he never texts me first. Not even on my birthday. He talks to me on Facebook sometimes, but I can tell he's doing something else at the same time. The thing is, I don't really know him anymore.

I knew him when I was seven and we lived together. But now he's just some stranger who shares my DNA. He likes me, I think, but he's got his own life. He's got a dad, and a girlfriend, and loads of mates. He doesn't need me.

I walked home slowly from the park, thinking about Lyn, my foster mother.

I liked Lyn a lot. She was young, and friendly, and kind. She listened to me when I talked to her, and laughed at my jokes. She gave me the schoolbag that Maddy liked, and took me to Lightwater Valley for my 14th birthday. Secretly, I wished I could stay with her for ever.

****

Lyn was still at work when I got home after the bus thing. I made myself a cup of tea and turned on the telly. I love kids' TV. And kids' films. Cartoons, the Disney Channel, Pixar films, all that little kid stuff. Cartoons have all the best jokes.

I'd been home about an hour when Lyn came in. She called "Hello!" and came into the living room.

"Hi, Clare," she said. "How's it going?"

"Fine," I said. I never knew what to say to Lyn. I liked her a lot, but she always made me feel a bit awkward. The whole foster family thing was weird. I was supposed to treat her like my mum, but she wasn't my mum. She was a stranger. So it was like our whole relationship was a lie, and I hate lies.

"Did you have a nice day?" Lyn asked. I shrugged.

"Yeah," I said. That was a lie. Now I was the liar. But I didn't want to tell Lyn what my day was really like. I didn't want to have to talk for ages about making friends and talking to the teachers. I just wanted her to leave me alone and let me watch *Blue Peter* in peace.

Lyn sat on the edge of my chair. She smiled at *Blue Peter* but she didn't say anything.

"What do you want for tea?" she said after a bit. "Fish and chips?"

"Sounds good," I said. It did. My old foster parents were all very keen on healthy food, but Lyn was like my dad. Fish finger sandwiches, and jacket potatoes, and beans on toast. It was one of the nice things about living with her.

"Do you want to do something tonight?" she said. "I know I should tell you to do your homework, but I've had a long day, and I'm not feeling very mum-y. We could watch a film, maybe?"

I shrugged again. When Lyn was nice to me it made me feel weird all over. It made me want to hide.

"I dunno," I said. I stared at the telly. "I'm sort of watching this."

Lyn sat there on the arm of my chair. She didn't speak or move. For a moment, I felt a bit guilty. It wasn't her fault. She was trying her best. I turned my head.

"Lyn ..." I said, but she was already halfway to the door.

She looked back, a little too fast. Her face was all hopeful.

"Yes?" she said.

I hesitated.

"Can I have sausage instead of fish?" I said. The hopeful look faltered a bit. Then she smiled.

"Course you can," she said, and left.

5. TRUTH OR DARE

Maddy was waiting at the bandstand the next day. I thought she might not be, but she was.

"Hello," she said, all shy. That made me feel better. I'd been so nervous, all day. What if she wasn't there? What if she didn't like me? But she was as nervous as I was.

"What do you want to do?" I asked. Maddy shrugged.

"This is your place, not mine," she said. "What do people do for fun here?"

I wasn't sure what she meant. My place? She'd lived here longer than I had.

"We don't do anything," I said. "We just do what everyone does. Hang out. Go round each other's houses. Watch TV and mess about on the internet."

I didn't go round to anyone's house here, of course. Because everyone at my school hated me.

"Can we go round to your house then?" Maddy asked.

I hesitated.

"I dunno ..." I said. "It's a bit boring. There isn't much stuff there." I wasn't sure what we would do at Lyn's house. Lyn would have taken her laptop to work. There weren't many DVDs. And I didn't have much stuff. Not cool stuff anyway.

"OK," said Maddy. "So ... what shall we do, then?"

We went and got ice creams from the stand in the car park.

"Don't you feel sorry for the people who sell ice cream in cold weather?" Maddy said. "I do. No one but me ever buys ice creams from them. I always think they look so lonely."

That made me smile. It was the sort of thing Lyn would say. She always bought lucky heather from gypsy ladies, and *Big Issues* from homeless people. She always stopped and talked to them too. I thought Lyn would probably like Maddy. Lyn talked lots when she was nervous too. Lots of people do, I've noticed. I wish I did. Then maybe I'd be able to talk properly to Lyn, instead of sitting there like a lemon.

Maddy and I talked to the ice cream man. His name was Joe, and he ran a chip van in winter and an ice cream van in summer. He gave us free sprinkles too.

There was an odd moment when we paid. Maddy handed Joe her money, and he gave her a funny look.

"You can't pay with this, love," he said.

He held up her 50p piece. It looked exactly like an ordinary 50p, but bigger and chunkier.

"That's weird," I said. I took the coin from Joe. "Where did you get that from, Maddy?"

"Oh ..." Maddy said. "It's just ... it's old money. She looked at the coin in my hand – an ordinary pound. Then she felt in her purse and took out a pound coin of her own.

She looked tense, like she'd made some sort of mistake and she was worried I was going to catch her out. But why?

After we'd eaten our ice creams, we went and said hello to the sad-looking goats and pigs in the petting zoo. We tried to feed them some crisps, but they weren't interested.

"Glad I'm not a goat!" said Maddy.

Then we went and sat on the swings. We swung back and forth, and gave the joggers marks out of ten for sexiness. Then we played Truth or Dare.

Truth or Dare was fun. Maddy always picked Truth and I always picked Dare. First, Maddy dared me to tell one of the joggers I fancied him. She dared me to climb over the fence in the petting zoo and touch the biggest pig in there. She dared me to nick one of the golf balls from the crazy-golf course. I did all of her dares except the last one. I tried, but the crazy-golf woman was looking, so I couldn't.

When it was my turn, I asked Maddy which famous person she fancied the most. She picked John Lennon from the Beatles. Then I asked her what she was most afraid of.

"Robert and Chris," she said, immediately. "And Liam and Andy and Craig."

"Who?" I asked. But her face went closed and sad.

"Boys at my children's home," she said. "I don't want to talk about them, thank you."

"Are you OK?" I said. She nodded.

"Yes," she said. "I'm fine, thank you. Your turn."

When it was my turn again, I asked her which real life person she fancied most, but she wouldn't say.

"What's the point?" she said. "You don't know any of the boys I know." So I asked her which person in this park she fancied most. She said Joe the ice cream man, and I nearly fell off my swing, I laughed so hard.

"What?" she said. "He was nice!"

"He was about 40!" I said.

"He's the only man I've talked to!" said Maddy. "I can't fancy someone I haven't talked to!"

But I thought that was a bonkers thing to say. I fancy loads of people I've never talked to.

"What about John Lennon?" I said. "You haven't talked to him."

But Maddy said that was different.

"I know who John Lennon is," she said. "I know all his songs off by heart."

"Yuck!" I said.

Maddy started singing.

"Help me if you can, I'm feeling down ..."

I knew that one. Lyn liked the Beatles. She liked to sing along to them when she did the washing-up. I joined in.

24

"Help me get my feet back on the ground.
Won't you ple-e-e-e-e-ease, help me-e-e-e?"

6. BEST FRIENDS

After that, Maddy and I met up every day after school. Maddy had to be back at her children's home at six, for dinner, so we had nearly two hours together. We hung out on the swings, and talked. Sometimes we went and shouted stuff at the boys on the skateboard ramps, but most of them were only about 11, so it was a bit boring. Sometimes we went into town and looked round the shops. We would buy magazines, and then read them out loud and giggle. It was something to look forward to, when the girls at school were being bitchy, or the boys on the bus were being awful.

I was starting to see why Maddy didn't have any friends at her school. She was a bit odd. She hadn't heard of any of the film stars the girls at school liked. She didn't watch any of the TV shows they watched, and she didn't listen to any of the music they listened to. It was bonkers. But sort of nice, too. Usually, I was the one who was left out.

I used to tease her about it.

"One Direction! You must have heard of One Direction!"

"Of course I have," she said. But she looked so awkward, I knew she was lying.

"What is it, then?" I said. I knew if I said, 'Who are they?' she'd guess they were a band.

"A TV show?" she said.

I laughed so much my stomach hurt.

"A TV show! Where do you live? Do you even have a TV? Do you even know what TV is?"

"I just don't watch telly that much!" she said. But she lived in a children's home! She went to school! Did she just not listen to anybody ever?

It was crazy, the people she'd never heard of. I started to wonder if she was really a kid at all. Perhaps she was secretly a 90-year-old lady who just looked like a 14-year-old girl.

"Justin Beiber?" I said. "Please tell me you've heard of Justin Beiber."

"Oh, I know him! He's this one, right?" Maddy held up one of her magazines. "He's … um … a singer?"

"Um … a singer? He's Justin Beiber! Are you from another planet?"

"Maybe," said Maddy, and she smiled at me. It was a very Maddy sort of smile. With Maddy, I was never sure if she was being serious, or not.

After a bit, she turned it into a game. I'd say a name, and she'd pretend she'd never heard of that person.

"Harry Potter!"

"He's a film star, right?"

"Harry Potter!" I yelled.

"Pop star?"

"Harry Potter! Everyone's heard of Harry Potter! Even my gran's heard of Harry Potter!"

"Nope," Maddy said. "Sorry. Are you making him up?"

She was joking, of course. Even Maddy had heard of Harry Potter.

I mean, of course she had.

Hadn't she?

"What do you do?" I said. "You don't watch telly, you don't watch films, you only listen to old music, and you don't mess about on the internet. So what do you do?"

Maddy shrugged. "I read," she said. "I walk. I think. I go places. I go places no one else knows about."

"Like where?" I asked, and Maddy smiled.

"Like here," she said, which was bonkers. We were in a park full of people! It wasn't exactly a secret.

"Oh yeah," I said. "The park! No one knows about the park!"

But Maddy only smiled.

7. LONELINESS

I hated being in care. It was like being on a tiny rocky boat without a rudder. You never stay still. You never feel safe. And you never know which way the wind is going to blow you. At least, I don't. I was in four different foster homes and one children's home before I came to live with Lyn, and I had to leave them all.

My first foster home was with a woman who was an emergency foster carer. I lived with her for two weeks when my mum went to prison. After that, I moved in with a family who had a lot of kids. Three birth kids, two foster kids, and me. I lived there for two years. The mum and dad were nice, but they were always busy. I always felt squashed by the other kids. Like there wasn't enough space. Like I was always about to get flattened. Or forgotten. Loads of my toys got broken. That was where the stone hedgehog that my gran gave me got stolen. Another kid took it and hid it for no reason at all.

In the end, my social worker said she thought I was getting a bit lost in that house, and I went to live with a smaller family. There was a mum, a dad, and their kid, Jack. I liked the family a lot. They were funny and kind. They took me to guitar lessons, and the pantomime, and on summer holidays in Devon. They sang silly songs in the car and taught me how to cook.

I lived with that family for three years. When I was 12, the dad got a new job and they moved to London. They didn't take me with them. I hated them for that. Hated them.

Next, I went to a lady who lived on her own. That was a disaster. She hated me and I hated her. Everything about her drove me crazy.

She was really strict about everything. She wanted me to keep my room SPOTLESS, ALL THE

TIME. And I'm just not very tidy. She'd ask me to do something and then want it done RIGHT NOW THIS MINUTE. And if I forgot to do it, she yelled at me. You have things in common with people you're related to. My brother Matt has the same sense of humour as I do. And we both support Newcastle United. And we look really similar. My dad and I had loads in common. We both loved the same films and TV shows. We even liked the same food – M&Ms, and jam doughnuts, and pepperoni pizza. I have things in common with my mum too. Like … long fingers. And blue eyes.

But I had nothing in common with that foster mum. She cooked horrible slimy food that I hated. She watched boring TV shows about DIY. I never thought any of her jokes were funny. I hated the clothes she bought me. She was like one of the girls at school, Catherine or Jade. We just didn't understand each other.

I lived with that lady for a year, then we both told my social worker it wasn't working. And that's when I went to live in a children's home.

The children's home was called Harrison House. I hated it. I hated everything about it.

I hated living with lots of other kids. I hated
how I never felt safe. I was always worried that
someone would hurt me, or try and steal my
things, or just come and push me around. I could
never relax.

I thought I was probably stuck there for
ever. But then at the end of the year, I came to
live with Lyn. Lovely, kind, friendly Lyn. But
I'd learned one thing, after all those moves. I'd
learned that it was a bad idea to like being
somewhere. It was a bad idea to start caring
about someone. Because I always had to go. And
when I went, it broke my heart.

8. HURT

The thing about Maddy was, she knew what that
felt like. Maddy was the only person I could
talk to about school. I told her all about Jade
and Catherine. I told her how horrible it was
to always have the wrong shoes, and the wrong
bag, and the wrong hair. She knew how horrible
it was to not have any friends. She didn't try
and come up with ways I could fix everything,
or tell me I should just try harder. She just ...
understood.

I even told her about my dad, and how much I miss him. I never talk about my dad. Ever. But I knew Maddy would understand. I showed her the little hedgehog Gran gave me, that used to be his.

"It's my most precious thing," I told her. She didn't laugh. She held it very carefully, like she knew how important it was.

"I don't have anything from my parents," she said. "I can't even really remember them. Not properly."

But she was odd. It wasn't just that she didn't know anything about stuff like TV and music. It was that she got so excited by totally ordinary things. Weeks after my phone got broken, Lyn bought me a new one and Maddy loved it. She loved all the games, and she loved the music, and she was always making me find her funny YouTube clips to watch. I showed her lots of the silly ones Lyn had shown me, and she loved them just as much as Lyn did.

"Haven't you ever seen the internet before?" I said. "Don't you have computers where you come from?"

"Oh yeah," said Maddy. "But they're always busy."

"You don't have your own laptop?" I said. Kids in care are all supposed to have their own laptop. Maddy looked a bit awkward.

"Oh ..." she said. "It broke." And then she changed the subject.

I found myself worrying about Maddy a lot. I worried about those boys she told me about, the ones she was afraid of. Did they break her laptop? Were they why she didn't have a phone, or MP3 player, or decent clothes? I used to look at her sometimes, with her ugly old coat that didn't fit, and her dark hair that always needed cutting, and I'd just want to take her home and adopt her. I know that's a weird thing to think about your best friend, but I did. I couldn't help it.

"Are you going to live with this foster mum forever?" she asked me.

"Dunno," I said. "Are you going to live at your children's home forever?"

"I expect so," Maddy said, sadly. "No one adopts kids my age. Do they?"

I didn't answer. I didn't have to. She was right.

No one did.

"What's the name of your children's home?" I asked her one day, about a month after we'd met.

"Milton Street," she said. "Why?"

"No reason," I said. But it got me thinking. As far as I knew, there were two children's homes around here – one for girls and one for boys. I'd never heard of Milton Street. Was Maddy making things up? And if so, why? Or was Milton Street some special children's home – for kids with behaviour problems, or learning difficulties, or something? Maddy was definitely a bit strange. But was she strange in a dangerous way?

I didn't think so. Maddy was weird. But she wasn't angry and fierce and furious, like some of the kids I've known. She was just ... odd.

When I went home, I typed 'Milton Street children's home' into Google. Nothing. I wasn't surprised. Most children's homes don't have websites. Next, I tried 'Milton Street' and my postcode. The street popped up – about half a mile away from where Lyn lived.

So that bit was real, at least.

****

And then one day, about a week later, I came into the park and found Maddy sitting on the bandstand with her head down.

"Hello," I said.

She didn't move.

"Maddy – hello!"

She looked up, and I gasped. She had a big black bruise all across one side of her face. Her tights were ripped, and there was a long bloody scrape all the way down her leg.

"What happened?" I said. "Maddy! Are you all right?"

"I'm fine," she said, and she turned her face away. I touched her arm. She flinched.

Maddy hardly ever talked about her home. I understood why. But this was serious. She was really hurt.

"No, you aren't fine," I said. I pulled up the sleeve of her coat. Her shirt was covered in blood. "Maddy!"

"It's fine," she said. "It's just a cut. Really." But she was nearly crying.

"What happened?" I asked. "Maddy? What happened to you? I'm your friend. Tell me."

Maddy didn't answer.

"Was it those boys?" I said. "Those boys at your children's home? It was, wasn't it?"

She nodded.

"I don't know why they're always after me," she said. "I haven't done anything!"

I knew why. Maddy stood out about a mile. I was pretty sure she'd get picked on if she went to my school. But I didn't think anyone would attack her.

"What do they want?" I asked. Maddy rubbed her eyes.

"Everything," she said. "Money. My stuff. I don't know. I hate them." She was almost crying. "They broke this girl's arm at school," she said. "I don't know why. I don't want to know. Nobody knew it was them, because the girl was too scared to tell. But they could have killed her. They would have killed her if she'd told, I bet. They wouldn't care."

"Maddy," I said. I felt sick. "You have to do something. You have to. You have to tell someone what's happening. Tell one of the carers. Or your social worker. Or – anyone."

Maddy gave a hiccuppy laugh.

"Other kids have tried that," she said. "They won't do anything. They never do. Never, never, never!"

9. YOU'RE NOT REAL

All the next day, I worried about Maddy. I shouldn't have let her go home, should I? I should have made her tell someone what was happening. 'I'll do better today,' I thought. 'I have to.'

I had a horrible day at school. Catherine and Jade were doing this thing where they just started giggling whenever they saw me. They didn't say anything, they just giggled like mad. In the end, I got so annoyed that I went and got a black marker from an English classroom. I marched over to them and drew black scribbles all over Jade's face and shirt before she could move. They both started screaming and yelling at me. Then they went and told Mrs Granger I'd been picking on them. They acted all innocent:

"We weren't doing anything!"

"Clare just attacked us for no reason!"

And then Mrs Granger gave me a half-hour-long lecture about how I had to 'respect my fellow pupils', while Catherine and Jade sat at the other end of the house block and giggled.

The kids on the bus thought it was so funny.

"Ooh, Clare, are you going to draw on me?"

"What's the matter, Clare? What's wrong with my face? Isn't it pretty enough for you?"

"Do you only like to draw on girls? Is it cos you fancy them? Do you fancy Jade Davidson, Clare? Do you?"

I squeezed my hands into tight fists, looked out of the window, and counted the minutes until I could escape.

When I got to the park, Maddy was waiting at the bandstand as usual. She was sitting on the steps drinking from a can of Coke. She didn't look up.

"Hey," I said.

Maddy didn't move. I started to get nervous. Was she angry with me?

"Maddy?" I said. At last she looked up. She was crying.

"Maddy! Are you OK? What's happened?"

Maddy shook her head.

"Maddy?"

"I'm afraid to go home," she whispered.

I sat on the steps beside her and put my arm around her.

"Is it those boys again?"

Maddy nodded.

"They're going to be waiting for me tonight." Her eyes were huge in her white little face. "I don't know what to do," she whispered.

I squeezed her.

"You should tell someone," I said. "Really, you should. One of your carers. Pick the nicest one and just tell them."

"I can't," said Maddy. She looked so afraid. "They won't do anything. They never do. And if those boys find out I told, they'll kill me."

"They won't kill you," I said. But I wasn't sure. I knew what kids were like. Kids in children's homes did all sorts of terrible things, and the carers never even guessed.

"Listen," I said. "I'll come with you. I'll tell the carers for you. I'll tell them I made you tell. Then it won't be your fault, will it?"

"You can't come," said Maddy.

"Why not?"

"Because."

"Because what?" I said.

"Because," said Maddy. She took a slow breath. "Because you're not real."

I opened my mouth and shut it again.

"What do you mean, I'm not real? Are you saying I'm a liar?"

"No ..." said Maddy. She looked like she wished she'd never said anything.

"So what are you saying?" I said. "Of course I'm real." I was really hurt. I'm not my real self with everyone. I pretend to be tougher than I am all the time. At home. At school. But with Maddy I was real. And she thought I was pretending.

Maddy saw my face. "I don't mean you're not real," she said. "I mean – none of this is." She waved her arm. "The park. These people. All that stuff you talk about, Justin Beiber and YouTube and camera phones. It's just ..." She shrugged. "It's a story," she said. "Or a dream. You're just a dream I'm dreaming."

I stared. I really, honestly did not know what she was on about. Was she mad? Or drunk, maybe? She didn't sound drunk. Maybe she was trying to be clever. 'The world's a dream.' It sounded like something my English teacher would say. 'All the world's a stage.'

But I didn't think Maddy was trying to be clever. She sounded like she really believed it. I wasn't real. The world wasn't real. It scared me, that she thought that.

"I'm not a dream," I said. "Maddy. Look at me. I'm real." I took her hands. They were cold. "Can you feel that?" I said. Maddy nodded. "And ..." I felt inside my schoolbag. I found my little stone hedgehog, took it out and gave it to Maddy. I wanted to give her something that really mattered. I thought that would show her how real I was. "There," I said. "Can you feel that?"

"Yes," Maddy said.

"So how can this be a dream?" I said. "I'm your friend, Maddy. I'm here. And I care about you. I worry about you."

I did. She looked so small and helpless in her ugly old coat, and with her old-fashioned hair that no one ever bothered to get cut. She squeezed my hedgehog so tight that her fingers went white. She was nearly crying.

"Maddy," I said, "let me come back with you. Please don't just go home. Please let me help."

Maddy shook her head.

"I can't," she said. "Don't! Please!"

I tried to take her hand, but she pulled away.

47

"Here," she said. She held out my hedgehog. I shook my head.

"Keep it," I said. "Just for the weekend. Give it back on Monday."

"OK," said Maddy. Her eyes filled with tears. I went to hug her, but she stood up and stepped away.

"I've got to go," she said. "I'll be late. I'm sorry!"

"Maddy!" I said. "Wait!" But she wouldn't look back.

10. ALONE

The next day was a Saturday. I never saw Maddy
at weekends. That weekend was awful. Lyn kept
wanting to do things – go for a walk, go shopping,
see a film. Any other time I'd have been pleased,
but right now it all seemed so unimportant. Also,
Lyn's hopeful face kept reminding me of Maddy,
the first time I'd met her. I couldn't stop thinking
about how much she'd wanted me to be her
friend. I worried about her the whole weekend.
What was happening to her? Was she safe? I
wished I'd given her my phone number. Perhaps
she wanted to talk to me and she didn't know
how to find me. I wondered about just going to

the park and seeing if she was around, but I knew she wouldn't be. Children's homes always make you do stupid art and cooking and sport and stuff on Saturdays. Or mine did, anyway.

'You're not real.' That's what she'd said. Why would she say something like that? Did she really believe that?

I felt so helpless and worried. I wished my dad was still alive, so I could ask him for help. He'd know what to do.

Because I was only six when my dad died, people think I don't remember him. But I do. I miss him so much. I miss watching the football with him on Saturday afternoons. I miss playing Skalextric with him and Matt. I miss talking to him. I miss just having someone in my life who I knew would never dump me.

In the end, even Lyn could see something was the matter. "Clare," she said. "Clare, is there something wrong? You seem so ... worried."

"I'm fine," I said. "Really, everything's fine."

"Is it school?" Lyn asked. "I know things have been a bit rough at school. Maybe I could talk to someone –"

"No!" I said. I didn't want Lyn to know about school. All those detentions, all that homework I never did, all those times I'd nearly punched Jade in the nose.

Lyn looked sad.

"Please let me help you, Clare," she said.

Then I had an idea.

"You could buy me new shoes," I said. "And pay for a haircut!"

Lyn looked a bit surprised.

"OK," she said. "Well, you've just got new shoes. But we can certainly do the haircut."

So we went to the nice hairdressers in town, and I got my hair cut short and spiked up. It looked utterly brilliant.

So that was something.

11. FEAR

On Monday, I waited for Maddy at the bandstand after school. I waited ten minutes.

20.

Half an hour.

An hour.

She didn't come.

I tried not to worry. Maybe she'd got held up at school. Maybe she was ill. She might have been ill.

But I didn't believe it.

Something terrible had happened to her, I knew it. Those boys at her children's home had done something awful. I should have tried harder on Friday, when she told me. I should have followed her home. I should have told Lyn.

I should have done something.

On Monday, I waited an hour.

On Tuesday, I waited two.

On Wednesday, I was still hopeful. Maybe she'd be there today.

She wasn't.

I had to do something. I didn't know what exactly, but something. I took out my phone and looked up the directions to Milton Street again. It was about ten minutes' walk from the park. I bit my lip. Did I dare just go up to the door and knock? What if Maddy didn't want to talk to me? Maybe she'd be angry with me for trying to find her. She was such a private person.

But if she really was in trouble, I had to help her. Didn't I?

I started walking. It was cold. It started to drizzle. The park was nearly empty. I took a shortcut through the hedge and walked down the main road. The cars swished past me, their headlights shining. The streetlights began to come on, one by one. Their yellow light reflected back in the puddles on the pavement. The sky was a deep, dark grey.

Milton Street was full of fancy Victorian houses. Bay windows, big front gardens, posh cars parked all along the road. I walked all the way up the street. There was no children's home. Not even a really well hidden one. Nothing.

At the end of the street was an old building. Something about it made me stop. It was another Victorian house, but there were lots of little details about it which made me wonder. The car park outside. The big industrial bins. The brass nameplate by the door. There were big modern-looking railings around the car park, and a gate with a buzzer to press to get in.

It looked like it might have been a children's home. A small one. But it also looked very, very empty. Really empty. I mean, there were boarded-up windows and everything.

I pushed the gate. It opened with a rusty *creeeak*. I went up to the house and peered through the one window that wasn't broken. The room inside was dark and bare. It might have been an office, long ago, but it hadn't been used for years. There was an old desk, and some old newspapers, and bare floorboards. Graffiti was sprayed on the walls.

I went up to the front door and tried the handle. It was locked, of course. But there was that little brass nameplate.

MILTON STREET CHILDREN'S HOME

This was it.

Did Maddy live here? How could she? I went around the side of the building, trying to find a back door. It was locked. I knocked as hard as I could, calling, "Maddy! Maddy!" No one answered. I didn't expect them to. I didn't really think Maddy was living there. I mean, it would explain why she didn't watch TV, or listen to music, or have the internet, but she looked too clean and tidy to be living in a place like this.

And if she was hiding out here, why would she tell me her real address?

But … I was baffled. If Maddy didn't live here, then where did she live? Was she lying about everything? I couldn't believe it. She'd sounded really, honestly scared when she talked about those boys. Maybe she was a good actor. But … it seemed such an odd thing to make up. And why would she lie about it? I lived with a girl once who used to tell lies all the time to make us feel sorry for her. But Maddy wasn't like that. She hardly talked about herself at all. I had to pretty much force her to say anything.

It was a mystery, and I hate mysteries. Nearly as much as I hate being lied to. And I really, really, really hate that.

I went through the gate onto the street. As I did so, something weird happened. I'm not sure exactly how to describe it. It felt a bit like static electricity, or an electric shock, or … well, I'm not sure what. But it was definitely weird.

I looked back. And then I saw it.

There was a different view. Just between the gateposts. To the right and left of the gate

I could see the old house with the boarded-up windows. But when I looked right between the gateposts, all the windows had glass in them. The door was painted red, with new paint. I could even hear voices. Someone singing, someone laughing. And there was a car parked in the car park.

Look. I know, OK? I know it sounds bonkers. It felt pretty bonkers at the time. But there, just between the gateposts, I could see it. The middle part of a car. And on either side of the posts, there was nothing.

I moved to the right. Now I could see the end of the car, through the gate. I moved to the left. Now I could see the front, but yes – just through the gate. I looked through the railings. No car. I looked through the gate. Car. What was going on? Was it a trick? Were there mirrors somewhere? Or magic? Or what?

I came closer to the gate. The air even smelled different here. I came closer again. Was it some sort of magic door? But to where? Another world? Another time?

I touched the gatepost. And then –

The car vanished.

The red door vanished.

The glass windows vanished.

All I could see was the old abandoned children's home. Peeling paint on the door. Boarded-up windows. Empty car park. Same as before.

I stared.

What just happened?

Was it real?

And what did it have to do with Maddy?

12. FOUND

I walked home in a daze.

'I have to tell someone,' I thought. 'I have to.'

I'm usually a really private person. But I'd got used to telling Maddy things. Silly things like which boys I liked. And important things like what Jade and Catherine did to me. I liked it, I realised. I liked having someone in my life who listened.

'I don't know what to do,' I thought. 'I need help.' Just thinking that made me feel so much better. 'I can't tell Maddy,' I thought. 'So I'll tell

Lyn. When I get home. I'll make her help me find Maddy.'

Lyn's car was in the drive when I got back. Good. I opened the door and called, "Lyn! Lyn!"

"In here!" Lyn replied. She was in the kitchen, mopping the floor. She looked up and saw my face. "What's the matter? What's happened?"

"I don't know," I said, and I told her. I told her everything. All about Maddy, and those boys, and how scared Maddy was. I even told her what had happened at the children's home. About the gate, and what I saw through it.

"I don't understand what happened," I said. "Maybe I'm going mad. I don't know. But Maddy was really scared. And someone really did hurt her. And I can't stop thinking about it."

Lyn was staring at me. Her face was white. She looked like she'd seen a ghost.

"I –" she said. She stopped. She handed me the mop. "Wait there," she said. And she left the room.

I stood in the middle of the kitchen floor, holding Lyn's mop. I felt ridiculous. But also oddly pleased. I didn't know what Lyn was going to do, but I was pretty sure she was going to help.

Lyn was ages. I was starting to wonder if I should go after her when I heard her footsteps on the stairs. She came up to me and held out her hand.

"What?" I said. "What is it?"

"I couldn't find it," said Lyn. "I thought I must have lost it. But I hadn't. Here. Take it." She took my hand and put something into it. Something small, and worn, and cold.

It was my stone hedgehog. The one my gran gave me. The one I gave to Maddy.

"But ..." I said. "How could you have my hedgehog? I gave it to Maddy."

"It's all right," said Lyn. "Don't be scared. I'm Maddy. Maddy's me. I used to come through that ... opening in the gate in Milton Street 20 years ago, when I was 14. I couldn't believe it, the first time. I thought I was going crazy. This whole other world, with everything different. Different shops. Different cars. And you. Can you see why I didn't believe you were real? I

could never decide what you were. Sometimes
I was sure you were really happening. And
sometimes I knew you were a dream."

I stared. I just stared.

"You're Maddy," I said. "You're Maddy!"

"I'm Maddy."

"But you can't be! You're Lyn! You're grown
up!"

"I know," said Lyn. "Sorry. It just sort of
happened."

"How can you be Maddy?" I said.

"I don't know," said Lyn. "I really don't. I
don't know why I came into the future when
I went through that gate, and other people
didn't. I didn't always. Sometimes I had to go
in and out ten or 20 times before it worked. The
universe is a huge and mysterious place, Clare.
Is it so surprising that sometimes it throws out
something unexpected like this?"

"I don't know," I said. I didn't. "But – I don't
understand. What happened to you? Why didn't

you come today? Or – I suppose it wasn't today for you. Why didn't you come 20 years ago?"

"I did what you told me," said Lyn. "I told the carers. They could see what had happened to me, of course. I told them I was afraid to stay in that home. They couldn't find new homes for five boys so fast, so they found a new home for me. I had to leave that night. I wanted to tell you what had happened, but how could I? You were 20 years away."

"Were they OK?" I said. "The people you went to?"

"Yes," said Lyn. "They were amazing." She hesitated. "In fact, they adopted me."

"They adopted you?"

Lyn nodded. "I couldn't believe it. I still don't, really. But it was a happy ending. A real, true, honest happy ending."

I just stared. I knew Lyn's parents, a bit. I'd met them twice. They seemed nice. I would never have guessed that Lyn was adopted. But then, why would I?

"You're Maddy," I said. Lyn nodded.

"I'm Maddy."

"But your name's Lyn." I still didn't believe it. Lyn was Maddy. Maddy was Lyn.

But I could sort of see it, all the same. Lyn had the same dark hair as Maddy. She was fatter than Maddy was, but her smile was the same. She talked to strangers just like Maddy did. She even liked the same music. John Lennon, and The Beatles.

"Lyn is short for Madelyn," Lyn said. "I stopped being Maddy when I was 16. I always hated that name. Maddy the Mad. I wanted to leave all that behind me."

"Did you recognise me?" I said. "When I came to live here. Did you know who I was?"

Lyn laughed.

"How could I?" she said. "I knew you for two months, 20 years ago. I didn't have any photographs of you. I didn't even know your surname. I wasn't even sure you were real. Well, I had the hedgehog. I knew that was real. But the rest of it was just so ... fantastical. I thought maybe I'd invented you." She smiled.

64

"Also, I remembered you as taller. And older. But – yes – I suppose you did always remind me of my old friend, a bit. But I never dreamed you were the same person."

"You're Maddy," I said, again.

"Yes," said Lyn. "Do you mind?"

I thought about it. It should have felt weird. It did feel weird. But it felt nice too. I'd known Lyn since she was 14. She'd known me for 20 years. That's longer than anyone has known me, when you think about it. Longer than my mum and Matt, even. I liked that.

And people don't change so much, really, do they? I thought about the person I was when I was eight ... or ten ... or 12. I'm different now in lots of ways, of course. But really, inside, I'm the same person now as I was then. In all the ways that matter, I'm the same.

"No," I said. "I don't mind. I like it."

"Good." Lyn looked pleased. "Because ... listen ... one thing I do remember is how unhappy you were. At school, I mean. Do you really hate it that much?"

"Oh …" I still didn't want to talk to Lyn about school. Except … I already had done, hadn't I? "School's OK," I said. Then, "I just haven't bothered trying to make friends, that's all. Because I don't know how long I'm going to stay here."

"Would you like to stay here?" Lyn asked.

I looked at the floor. Of course I wanted to stay there. How could she not know that? Shouldn't she just know that, without me having to say?

But why should she know? I'd been pretty horrible to her, hadn't I, really? I thought about Maddy, with her white little face and her funny hair and her old-lady coat. I wouldn't expect Maddy to just know something about me without me telling her first. So why should Lyn be any different?

Because Lyn scared me. How much I liked Lyn scared me. Even now, I was still scared. Scared that she'd leave me.

But I wasn't scared of Maddy, was I? I trusted Maddy. Didn't I? Yes, I did.

Maddy always understood me.

And Maddy was Lyn.

Maybe Lyn would understand me too, if I gave her the chance.

I looked up at Lyn. I could see Maddy's face in her face. Her eyes were Maddy's eyes. Hopeful, and a little bit scared. I wondered if maybe Lyn might still need someone to look after her, just like Maddy did.

"Yes," I said. "I want to stay. If you want to have me, I want to stay."

But I knew she wanted me. I knew she always had. I knew what her answer was going to be, before she'd even opened her mouth.